Ruby
Fairy Tales

GEM CLASSICS LIBRARY

Retold by Jane Carruth

RAND McNALLY & COMPANY
Chicago • New York • San Francisco

Contents

The Elves and the Shoemaker

THERE WAS once a shoemaker who, through no fault of his own, found himself with scarcely any money.

"I don't mind that we have grown so poor," he said to his good wife, "for we can manage on very little. But the truth is that I have only enough money left to buy leather for one more pair of shoes."

His wife was a plump, cheerful woman who seldom let things get her down and who loved her husband dearly.

"Don't fret, my dear," she said. "Go to the market. Spend what money is left on good leather and make the shoes."

The shoemaker did as she suggested. He went to the market and spent the last of his money on a piece of fine leather. Then, as he was tired from his journey, for he was no longer young, he sat down by the roadside and had a rest before returning home.

On seeing his pale face and how wearily he entered his little workshop, his wife quickly brought him something to eat.

"Cut out the shoes tonight, husband," she said. "But leave the stitching of them until the morning. It is time you went to bed."

So the shoemaker cut out the shoes and left them on his workbench. Then he followed his wife upstairs to bed. Little did he know that, as he slept, the workshop door opened silently and in skipped two little elves. They hopped onto his bench and examined the leather. Then, exchanging twinkling glances but not saying a word, they set to work, stitching and hammering busily.

When the old man awoke in the morning he resolved, as he dressed, that he would put all his skill into the making of his final pair of shoes. There was a sad smile on his careworn face as he entered his workshop, for he was certain that it would be for the last time. What would happen next, he didn't dare to think.

He was just going to pick up his tools when he saw, to his amazement, that the leather he had cut out the night before had been made into a fine pair of shoes. There they sat on the bench – just asking to be picked up. And this the shoemaker did, holding them nervously in his hands and turning them this way and that.

"Bless my soul!" he exclaimed. "I've never seen finer shoes."

Excited now, he called his wife, and she too exclaimed over the fine stitching.

"They are so neatly made," she said at last, "so delicately stitched and yet so strong that they are sure to fetch a good price. Let's hope a customer comes in soon."

As it happened, the shoemaker did not have long to wait for his first customer – one of the richest merchants in the town.

"I am looking for something special," the merchant said. And then his eyes lighted on the shoes. "Yes, yes, these are just what I want, and I'm willing to give more than the usual price for them.".

The purchase was soon made and the delighted shoemaker found that he now had enough money to buy leather for two pairs of shoes. Once again he hurried off to the market and when he returned with two fine pieces of leather, one black and the other blue, he set to work at once to cut out the shoes.

"Leave it all there," advised his wife, after he had spent some time in his workshop. "There will be time enough in the morning to do the stitching – if it is necessary."

The shoemaker slept as soundly as usual but in the morning he confessed to his wife that he could not help feeling excited.

"It is just that I do not know what to expect," he explained as he prepared to go downstairs. "But surely it would be too much to hope that my work has already been done for me again."

No sooner did the shoemaker enter his workshop than he knew! For there on the bench were two pairs of exquisitely made shoes.

"There is no doubt," he exclaimed, turning to his wife as she followed him into the room, "that this is the work of a craftsman. I just could not do such fine stitching."

That day the shoes were sold for a very large sum and the shoemaker rushed straight off to market. He bought enough leather for four more pairs of boots and shoes before returning home.

"What must I do, wife?" he asked. "Shall I cut out the leather and leave it as usual on the bench? Or shall I try to make at least one pair of shoes before the light fails?"

"Leave it all where it is," said his wife. "Come and have a bite of supper and then we'll go to bed."

That night the little elves once more crept into the shoemaker's workshop and set to work hammering and stitching. They said nothing to each other as they worked, but they whistled softly and one would occasionally stop his labors to dance a jig in the moonlight. The shoes finished, they cleared up the workshop and left it neat and tidy.

The next morning the shoemaker's delight at finding the shoes and boots, all superbly made, waiting for him on the bench, was such that he almost wept for joy.

Long before the morning was over he had sold all four pairs and each for such a vast sum that he could hardly credit his good fortune.

"With all this money," he told his wife, "I will be able to buy a large store of leather."

"And with the help of your invisible shoemakers," laughed his wife, "you will be able to save for our old age."

Well, the shoemaker did buy a store of fine leather and each night he left two or three cut pieces on the bench. Every morning he would find two or three pairs of finely made shoes.

After a month or so, word of the shoemaker's exquisite shoes spread all round the county. High-born ladies and rich, over-fed lords crowded into his humble workshop begging for the favor of having a pair of shoes or boots made especially for them.

The shoemaker treated all his customers exactly alike although, it must be admitted, his price to the widows and the shopkeepers he had known all his life was still very low.

Sometimes in the quiet of the evening when the shoemaker had

pulled down the shutters, he would settle down by the fire and ask his wife to sit with him.

"It would be nice, husband," his wife said on one such evening, "if we could do something for our unknown helpers."

"It would be nice," repeated her husband thoughtfully, nodding his head. "Here we are with no more fears for the future – thanks to them . . ." he broke off, then added, "whoever they may be . . ."

"Christmas is coming in a week or so," said his wife. "And Christmas is a time of giving, so why don't we give presents to those who have helped us to our good fortune?"

"Why not indeed!" exclaimed her husband. Then he added, "But what shall we give them – we do not know who they are."

"Ah," went on his wife, her eyes shining with excitement. "But there is nothing to stop us finding out and I have an idea. This very night we will hide in the workshop and keep watch."

The shoemaker hesitated but when he saw how anxious his wife was to carry out her plan, he finally agreed. And so that night, the couple crept down to the workshop a few minutes before midnight and hid behind a tall cupboard.

They didn't have to wait long, for just as the clock began striking twelve, in came the two nimble little elves. They seated themselves on the shoemaker's bench, took hold of the leather that was cut out, and with their tiny fingers began to hammer and stitch.

They worked so swiftly and with such skill that the shoemaker had to cover his mouth with his hand to prevent himself from calling out in admiration. But he managed to remain silent, and the two elves worked on undisturbed. They did not stop for an instant until the shoes were finished. Then, without a word to each other, they placed the shoes neatly on the bench and hopped away.

"Did you see that?" exclaimed the shoemaker's wife, coming out from behind the cupboard. "Did you see that?"

"I did, of course I did," said her husband. "And sorry I was for those two little elves. They were so poorly dressed – and in this bitter winter weather too."

"That's what we can give them to show our gratitude!" cried his wife. "I shall make them warm undershirts and sweaters and socks for Christmas. And you can make them some tiny shoes."

That night, the good-hearted couple did find it difficult to sleep

for they were so busy planning their gifts. And in the morning the shoemaker's wife brought out her big bag of colored wools and her knitting needles. Her husband, meanwhile, began cutting out two tiny pairs of shoes and he used the finest and the gayest leather he could find for his work.

How happy they were that night and all the other nights before Christmas for now, at last, they could show how grateful they were to the two little elves.

The wife made soft pink undershirts and bright sweaters, one striped in colors of blue and white and the other in red and white. Long stripy stockings came next and she knitted them as best she could. Finally she made two jaunty knitted caps and two pairs of tiny mittens. "There is nothing so warm as mittens for the winter," said she confidently, when her husband burst out laughing at the sight of them. But then she had her own back when he showed her the two pairs of tiny leather trousers which he had cut and stitched with such patient care.

"They only look big enough to fit a doll!" she laughed. "But never mind – we've made those two kind-hearted little men gifts they will find most useful."

When the presents were ready, the shoemaker and his wife waited until just before midnight. Then, once again, they crept down to the workshop, but tonight instead of leaving out the leather, the shoemaker spread out the gifts, covering the bench with them. Then he joined his wife behind the tall cupboard and waited, for they were anxious to see what the little men would do.

At the first stroke of midnight in came the two elves. It was clear they were all ready to start work, but when they saw the undershirts and the sweaters and the woolen stockings, they just stared and stared at them as if they did not know what to do.

Then – all of a sudden – one little elf pulled on the stockings while his companion pushed his head through the neck of a sweater. In the next moment, they broke into high-pitched giggles and – half-dressed – they began hopping delightedly all over the bench.

The shoemaker squeezed his wife's hand as the elves began to dress themselves properly, stroking each article of clothing and admiring it before finally putting it on. When they were fully dressed, they clasped hands and began to sing.

"Now that we are so smart and fine,
Our cobbling work we must resign."

Then they began skipping and dancing over the chairs and the table until at last they skipped happily right out of the door.

"What did they mean, husband?" asked his wife, as the couple came out of their hiding-place.

"It means that our two little friends won't be back," said the shoemaker. "We have seen the last of them. But their delight in our presents is something I will never forget."

The shoemaker, of course, was right. The elves never did return. But, by now, he was so famous that he could sell shoes without any trouble. And the shoes he made himself were, strange to say, just as good as the ones made by his elfin cobblers. So the couple prospered and lived very happily to the end of their days.

The Donkey Cabbages

THERE WAS once a bold, handsome young hunter who had the great misfortune to fall in love with a witch's daughter. Now this hunter had in his possession a wonderful, magic wishing-cloak which granted him a wish whenever he wore it.

You may be sure it didn't take the witch long to find out about this cloak and as soon as she heard about it, she wanted it for herself.

One day she said to her daughter, "I have thought of a plan to get hold of that wishing-cloak for ourselves."

The girl loved the bold young hunter very much and would not willingly have done him harm. But she was also very afraid of her mother. So she nodded her head and asked what the plan was.

"You must be sitting at the window," her mother continued, "when next he calls at the house. Try and look very sad and keep your eyes fixed on the Garnet Mountain."

"I will do what you ask, mother," said the girl obediently. "But you must tell me what you have in mind for me to do."

"Patience, child," said the old witch. "When your love asks why you gaze towards the mountains and why you look so sad, you

17

must tell him that you long to go to the Garnet Mountain and to gather the precious stones which are scattered about its slopes."

"But, mother," protested the girl, "the mountains are wild and lonely and so steep and craggy that nobody goes there. Many, I know, have tried to get the stones and all have perished."

"You forget the wishing-cloak," said the old witch, with a cunning smile. "Your hunter will take you there by means of his wishing-cloak. Gather the finest and largest of the stones and then offer him wine I will give you for him to drink. The wine will contain a sleeping powder which will make him drowsy. As he sleeps, take the cloak from him and wish yourself home."

The girl was too much in the witch's power to defy her although she hated the whole plan. So the next day, when the hunter called upon her as usual, he found her sitting at the window and gazing towards the mountains.

"I have a great desire to gather some of the precious stones that are found only on the Garnet Mountain," she told him. She sighed and managed to look so miserable and sad that he put his arms about her to comfort her.

"My dear," he said, after a moment's silence, "there is nothing I

would not give you or do for you." And he pulled out his wishing-cloak, wrapped it about him and drew her underneath. Then he wished himself on the Garnet Mountain and, in a twinkling of an eye, they were standing on its slopes.

The witch's daughter pretended great joy as she began picking up some of the largest and finest of the precious stones that lay everywhere on the mountain-side. Then when the pockets of her apron were weighed down with the jewels, she took out a small flask of wine which her mother had given her.

"It is time to rest now," she said to the hunter. "Refresh yourself from this flask of wine and then take some rest."

The hunter took a long drink and then lay down. Almost at once his eyes closed and he fell into a drugged sleep. On seeing how deeply he slept, the girl went to him and carefully removed the cloak. Then, with a last look at her sleeping love, she put the magic cloak round her own shoulders and wished herself home.

Dawn was breaking when the hunter awoke and immediately he looked around for his sweetheart. There was no sign of her and his wishing-cloak was also missing. He had been betrayed.

"Fool that I am!" he cried aloud with great bitterness. "I have lost

my most precious possession and the only girl I have ever loved."

Then he began to imagine how the old witch and her daughter would be gloating over his loss, and he vowed that should he ever escape from the mountain, he would get his revenge.

As he lay there, too sick at heart to attempt to climb down the perilous slopes, two giants, who lived in the forest, came along.

At the sight of the young man lying on the ground, his eyes shut, the first giant raised one huge foot ready to step on him and crush him like a beetle. But the second giant said, in a good-natured way, "That little earthworm is scarcely worth the trouble of crushing. If we leave him alone he will die anyway, and if he has courage enough to struggle to the summit – well, the clouds will carry him away. So why bother about him? Come on, let's be on our way."

"You're right, brother," said the first giant. And he stepped over the huntsman and followed his companion.

The hunter sighed with relief when he saw the giants stride away. "I dare not risk another encounter with such monsters," he told himself. "Next time I might not be so lucky. So why not climb to the summit and let the clouds carry me away from here?"

With that, he got to his feet and began the long, hard climb to the mountain's summit. Once at the top he found that it was easy enough to jump onto one of the billowy, white clouds that drifted past in endless succession.

The cloud he had chosen floated him through the heavens in a slow, steady fashion, and the hunter lost all count of time. Suddenly, without warning, the cloud began to fall gently earthwards. Lower and lower it sank, and the young man scarcely knew whether to take his chance and jump or stay where he was. But before he could finally make up his mind, he discovered that the cloud was hovering just above a great patch of cabbages.

Thankfully he jumped clear and looked about him. The huge vegetable garden was surrounded by high walls, and growing everywhere – right up to the walls – were cabbages. Nothing but cabbages, cabbages and more cabbages!

Now the hunter had no great love for the taste of cabbages, especially raw ones, but he was desperately hungry, and if that was all that grew in this strange garden, then cabbages it would have to be. So he broke off some leaves and began to eat.

As he munched, he thought, "What cruel misfortunes have befallen me since I first loved that witch's daughter! Here am I, marooned in a cabbage patch, as hungry as a hunter can be, and forced to eat cabbage leaves like some animal."

He had scarcely taken a dozen mouthfuls, however, when something very strange began to happen to him.

He found that he had grown four legs; his head was large and hairy, and the ears that sprouted from it were big – far bigger than they had any right to be! And he had even grown a tail!

"Well, this is a fine state of affairs," said the young man to himself for he dared not speak aloud. "I eat an innocent-looking cabbage and I change into a donkey. There must be some black magic in this, somewhere!"

But now he was hungrier than ever for he had a donkey's appetite to satisfy. So he moved clumsily away to another patch of cabbages, which grew close to the wall, and went on munching.

He found the leaves of these cabbages much to his liking and he ate with enjoyment, finishing plant after plant. All of a sudden, he once again felt something very strange happening to him.

His head was shrinking and so too were his ears. His four donkey legs were no more and instead he had his own two human ones safely back. In short, he was a man again – and very relieved to find that not even a single hair of the donkey remained on his body.

"Well, that was a strange experience!" he said aloud. "These must

be donkey cabbages – some with the power to change the eater into a donkey and others to restore him to his former shape.''

And for the first time since he had left the mountain he broke out into loud laughter. "I may not have my wishing-cloak," he chuckled. "But I have something now which is almost as good. These cabbages will help me take my revenge on that treacherous old witch and her faithless daughter.''

And still smiling broadly, the hunter broke off one head from the cabbages that grew close to the wall and another from the cabbages he had first eaten. Then he climbed over the high wall and set off for the witch's house.

It took him several days to make the journey but when he was within sight of the house, he took cover in the woods. There he changed his clothes and stained his face with the juice of some berries so that the witch and her daughter would not recognize him.

When he was satisfied that this disguise was complete, he went to the witch's back door and knocked upon it loudly.

"What do you want, beggar man?" the witch demanded.

"I am no beggar," said the hunter. "I am on my way to the royal palace with two very special plants which the King has commanded me to grow for him. They are the most beautiful-tasting cabbages under the sun."

The witch's eyes glinted greedily when she heard this.

"They must indeed be wonderful if a King sends for them," she said in quite a different tone. "Come in, dear sir, and let me give you some refreshment."

As the hunter sat at the table, the witch hovered about, plying him with food. Then she said, "I don't suppose you would let me glimpse these wonderful cabbages?"

"Why not, madam!" said the young man. And he took from his pouch the two cabbage heads.

The witch stared at them enviously. "You couldn't perhaps spare me a leaf or two?" she began. "I have a new recipe which requires that the leaves of the cabbage be perfectly formed."

"I don't see why not," said the hunter innocently, and he broke off several leaves from the donkey cabbage he held in his right hand.

Suspecting nothing, the witch carried the leaves carefully into the kitchen and began immediately to prepare the dish. When it was ready, she was so greedy that she took a mouthful of the cabbage before even setting it down on the table. Scarcely had she swallowed it, however, than she changed into a donkey! Horrified, she ran, braying, into the courtyard.

The little maidservant came into the kitchen shortly afterwards, and seeing that she had the place to herself, she thought she would taste the delicious-smelling dish. Immediately after the first mouthful she too turned into a donkey and clattered away to join the old witch outside.

Meanwhile the witch's pretty daughter had come into the parlor to speak with the visitor. "I cannot think what has happened to my mother," she said. "I must go into the kitchen and find her."

"Let me go," said the stranger gallantly. And he got up and went quickly into the kitchen. There, he picked up the dish of cabbage leaves and was back in a moment.

"I saw nothing of your mother," said he. "But there is the dish she has prepared for you. Taste it and see if it is to your liking."

Smiling shyly, the girl accepted the dish and took a mouthful of the cabbage salad. No sooner had she done so than, like the others, she changed into a donkey and trotted out of the room.

Now that he had taken such complete revenge on those who had

betrayed his trust, the hunter was satisfied. He marched through the deserted house until he found the bathroom. He washed the stain from his face and combed his hair so that he once again became the handsome young hunter. Then he went down into the court-yard where the three donkeys stood dejectedly together.

"You are justly punished," he cried, and seizing a length of rope, he bound them together and drove them into the road.

He stopped at the first mill he came to and summoned the miller. "I have here three donkeys," he said. "They are difficult to manage and I propose giving them to you as a gift but it must be on my own terms."

"And what may these be, young sir?" asked the miller, scratching his head and looking at the hunter in some astonishment.

"The old donkey must be given only one meal a day," said the hunter, "and beaten three times though not too harshly. The second donkey must have two meals and only one daily beating. And the young pretty donkey must be given three meals a day and . . ." here the young man paused. Somehow he could not bear to think of

his former sweetheart enduring even the lightest of beatings. "No beatings for her," he continued. "Treat her very gently indeed."

The miller – greatly pleased at his good fortune – promised that he would carry out the young man's instructions. And well pleased with himself, the huntsman returned to the witch's house and found there everything he needed for his comfort.

At the end of the week he decided to return to the mill to find out how the donkeys were getting on.

"Bad news, sir," said the miller, when he saw him. "The old donkey was so bad-tempered and obstinate that she made life impossible for herself. Despite the beatings I gave her she would not work and she would not eat. In short, good sir, she died."

"And what of the others?" enquired the hunter.

"Oh, they are obedient enough," said the miller. "But come and see them for yourself."

At the sight of the two little donkeys standing side by side and looking the picture of misery, the hunter was full of pity.

"I have changed my mind about leaving them here," he told the miller. "Let me have them now and I will pay you well for the trouble you have taken to carry out my instructions."

The miller accepted the gold piece gratefully, for truth to tell he had found the donkeys a great nuisance. So the hunter drove them out into the road and back to the witch's house. His pity for them now was so real that he forgot all his former angry feelings and the wrong that had been done to him.

With trembling hands he brought out the second cabbage head from his pouch and, dividing it in two parts, fed the donkeys with it. Immediately they took on their former human shapes.

The serving girl who had, it must be confessed, brought about her own downfall by her greed, ran upstairs immediately to make the beds and tidy the rooms.

But the witch's beautiful daughter fell on her knees before the hunter and begged his forgiveness. "I had no wish to deceive and trick you," she said. "Everything I did was against my will for I truly love you, but my mother held me in her power and I had to do what she told me."

And gazing into her eyes, the hunter saw that she spoke words of truth. All his old love for her flooded into his heart and when she said to him, "Your wishing-cloak hangs in the cupboard and is waiting for you," he knew that she had placed herself in his power.

"I have no use for the cloak now," he said tenderly. "Let it hang there until we make a wish together for I intend to marry you."

So the witch's daughter and the young hunter were married, and so happy were they in their married state that they had no need of a magic cloak to make their wishes come true.

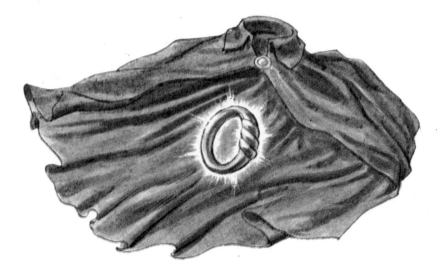

The Witch and the Children

ONCE UPON a time there was a poor woodcutter whose two children – a boy and a girl – were twins. As so often happens, when their mother died, the woodcutter married again, hoping that his new wife would run the house for him and take good care of his children.

It soon became clear, however, that his second wife found housework very boring and the twins a great nuisance. As often as she dared, she sent them off to see their grandmother. But fond as the old lady was of them, she believed that the proper place for the children was at home and so she only kept them a little while.

Soon the woodcutter's wife became quite desperate to rid herself of the twins for they meant extra work for her. So one morning she sent for them.

"I, too, have a granny," she told them, in the sweetest voice she could muster. "And it would give her great pleasure if you were to go and visit her for a little while. She lives in a dear little house in the middle of the forest and she will treat you very well if you do everything she says."

The children were too scared of their stepmother to ask any questions. Instead they watched silently while she packed a little bag with some of their clothes. She told them what path they must take through the forest in order to get to her granny's cottage. Then she kissed each of them on the cheek and waved them goodbye.

As soon as they were out of her sight, Martin – that was the boy's name – said, "Let's go and see our own granny first. We can tell her where we are going. I'm sure she would like to know."

So, instead of going straight into the forest, the children went along the road which led to where their grandmother lived.

The old lady was just baking bread when they arrived and after she had kissed them lovingly and given them something to eat, she asked why they had come so unexpectedly to see her.

"We are really on our way to stay with our stepmother's granny," Martin explained. But when the old lady heard this, she was greatly alarmed.

"You poor innocent children!" she cried in distress. "Your stepmother is not sending you to her granny. She is sending you to a wicked witch who lives in the darkest part of the forest!"

"What shall we do?" asked Martin. "We dare not go back home so soon!"

"If I kept you here it would only mean trouble for your father,"

said their grandmother. "So you must go. But listen to me carefully and do everything I say. You must be polite to the old witch no matter how much she scolds you. Will you remember that? And never say a cross word to anybody or any animal she keeps about the place."

"We will remember," said the poor twins in one voice.

"And don't eat anything she gives you," went on the old lady. "I will give you all the food you need for the time being."

She went to her cupboard and brought out a loaf of bread, a bottle of milk and a piece of ham, which she divided carefully between them.

The children took the food gratefully and, after taking a fond farewell of their true grandmother, they set out together for the witch's cottage in the heart of the forest.

It was so gloomy and dark in the middle of the forest, and the gnarled trees grew so closely together that they might have walked right past the weird little house if Martin had not seen the thin gray smoke curling up from its one twisted chimney.

"I wonder what she will be like?" his sister whispered, as they approached the door. "Will she have red eyes do you think?"

The witch was the ugliest old hag imaginable. She had a crooked back, long wispy hair that straggled over her thin shoulders and eyes that were a smoldering red. They seemed to burn right into the twins as soon as she opened the door to them.

"Good-day to you," said Martin politely. "Our stepmother has sent us to stay with you for a little while."

"Yes," said his sister, trying not to show that she felt so frightened. "She said you will treat us kindly if we do what you say."

"Well, sit down and listen to what I have to say," snarled the old witch, and she pushed the children down onto the floor so roughly that Martin felt like saying something rude. But he remembered his grandmother's words just in time, so he kept silent.

"You'll work for me as long as you are here," the old witch told

them, and she scowled down. "In fact, you'll start right away."

"She is a witch all right," Martin whispered, when the old woman had left the room. "Whatever shall we do?"

"We must try to remember what our granny told us," his sister whispered back. "Perhaps we shall find a way to leave."

The twins sat without moving on the bare wooden floor until the witch came back. She had a sieve in one hand and a bag filled with wool in the other.

"Now then," she began. "You, boy, take this sieve. Go down to the well and fill it with water. And you, girl, go into the corner over there. Sit at the spinning wheel. I want this wool made into yarn."

Martin carried the sieve out of the hut, thinking miserably to himself, "How can I fill this with water when it is full of holes!"

And as his sister went over to the spinning wheel, she was thinking, "How can I spin all this wool when I do not even know how to spin!"

Then she thought of the old witch and how terrible her anger would be when she discovered she had failed in her very first task, and she burst into tears.

As she sat there weeping bitterly, suddenly, out of all the nooks and crannies and from behind the long wooden bench, a whole host of little mice appeared. They pattered about the floor in an orderly manner until one of them – almost the plumpest – with a fine set of long whiskers, boldly went up to the weeping girl's feet.
"Little girl, little girl," he said, "why do you weep?"

Truth to tell, she was not exactly weeping at that moment, for the sight of so many little mice all appearing at the one time had so surprised her, she had almost forgotten her troubles.

"I – I can't spin," she said, after a moment's hesitation. "And I'm terribly, terribly frightened of the old witch who lives here. I don't know what she will do when she comes back."

"If you will give us some of your bread," said the plump mouse, "we will do your spinning for you."

"You can have all the bread my grandmother gave me," cried the girl thankfully, "if only you will do the spinning for me." And she scattered the bread on the floor.

Then the mouse chief said, "We would like to help you to escape, too. While we are spinning, go and search for the witch's cat. She is very fond of ham; and if you give her what you have, she will show you the way through the forest."

So the girl went out into the yard to look for the cat, but nowhere could she find it. After she had looked everywhere she could think of, she ran down to the well. There was her brother sitting on the low wall, a hopeless expression on his face.

"Every time I dip this stupid sieve into the water," he said, "all the water runs through the holes. I can't possibly fill it."

As he spoke, a number of little birds fluttered down to the

ground. "Give us some of your crumbs," chirped one, "and we will tell you how to fill your sieve with water."

So the boy took the bread his grandmother had given him, broke it into little pieces and scattered the crumbs on the ground. The little birds pecked away eagerly, chirping, "Fill the holes of the sieve with clay. Then you will be able to draw water from the well."

When Martin had done what the birds had said, he found that his sieve would indeed hold the water. Followed by his sister, he went back to the cottage carrying it carefully filled to the brim.

"Oh, there you are!" his sister cried as they slipped back quietly into the room. "Pretty, pretty pussy. Look what I have for you!"

And she took out the ham her grandmother had given her and gave it to the cat. Grateful for such a feast, the cat gave her a handkerchief and a comb.

"I will tell you how to find your way through the forest," she purred. "But when the witch comes after you, as she certainly will, then you must throw down the handkerchief and run."

"I will do that," the girl promised. "But what will it do?"

"The minute the handkerchief touches the ground it will become a wide lake," went on the cat. "But if the witch manages to get across and still follows you, then throw the comb behind you. When it touches the ground a thick hedge of brambles will spring up at once. It should be enough to hold the witch back while you make your escape.''

Just as the cat stopped speaking, the witch came into the room. She wanted to see if the twins had done the tasks she had set them.

She scowled ferociously when she saw that all the spinning was done and that Martin's sieve was filled to the brim with water.

''I see you have done what I told you to do,'' she admitted grudgingly. ''You can have a crust to eat if you like.''

But the children quickly said they had some milk to drink and were not hungry, although they were really rather tired. The witch's red eyes glinted spitefully with annoyance when she heard this, for once the children had eaten her food they would have been her servants forever. However, she said nothing, but threw some straw on the floor and told them that was where they would sleep.

''In the morning,'' she growled, as she prepared to leave them, ''I will have more work for you to do.''

The twins comforted each other as they lay in the coarse straw.

''At least we have the handkerchief and the comb,'' said the little girl.

''And the cat is our friend,'' said the little boy, reassuringly.

''If I have to spin again, the mice will help me,'' said the girl.

''And if I have to get water, the birds will help me,'' said the boy.

And then they put their arms about each other and pretended that they were going to sleep.

The old witch came to them at daybreak.

"Here's more wool to spin," she said roughly to the girl. "And, you, boy, go outside and chop my wood."

But no sooner had she left the room than the twins decided now was the time to make their escape. They ran and they ran – oh how they ran – out into the dark forest and along the first path they came to. And while they were running, the good-hearted cat sat quietly by the spinning wheel.

Before long the old witch came hobbling along, outside the hut. When she reached the little window she raised herself to have a look inside. But the window was too high for her to see in, so instead, she called out, "How is the weaving going, child?"

And the little cat answered, "It is going very well, thank you."

Satisfied, the witch hobbled off. But soon she was back again.

"How is the weaving, child?" she called out once more.-

And the cat answered, "It is going very well, granny dear. In fact, it is all but finished."

Now the witch knew that the spinning could not be finished so early in the day, and with a loud screech of rage she ran inside the house. Imagine her fury when she found her cat sitting beside the spinning wheel – and the girl nowhere to be seen!

"You let them go!" she shrieked at the cat. "You are mine, mine! And you let them go! Miserable creature, why did you let them escape?" And she hit the cat with her broomstick.

But the cat arched her back and hissed at her, "Yes, I let them go. For years I have served you and you never as much as threw me a fish-head. But these two dear children gave me their ham."

The witch realized she would get no help from her cat, so she rushed into the yard and called out to the birds, "Where are the children? Which way did they go?"

But the birds told her, "For years we have brought cheer to this miserable place with our song, yet never a crumb have you thrown to us. But these two dear children gave us the last of their bread. No, we will not tell you which path they took."

"I will catch them for myself," the witch snarled. "I don't need your help." And, mounting her broomstick, she set off after them.

The children had kept on running and running through the dark forest, never stopping for a moment, even to draw breath. But soon the witch was close behind them and they knew that no matter how fast they ran, they were no match for her and her broomstick.

"Listen, sister," panted Martin at last, and he tugged at his sister's arm to make her stop. "Listen, can you hear anything?"

"I can hear the sound of swishing and swooshing," said his sister, and she looked back over her shoulder.

"It's the old witch on her broomstick," said her brother. "She must be gaining on us. What shall we do?"

"I'll throw down the handkerchief the cat gave me," said the girl.

No sooner did the handkerchief touch the ground than it made a deep wide lake that stretched out behind them. Martin cried thankfully, "Ah, that will stop the old witch! Her broomstick won't carry her across all that water!"

But it didn't take the witch very long to go all the way round the lake, and although it wasted a bit of time, she was not so very far behind the children as they left the forest.

"Can you hear anything now?" Martin asked his sister. "We have only this broad meadow to cross and then we shall be home."

"I can hear the swishing and the swooshing of the witch's

broomstick again," cried his sister anxiously. "We must try to run faster or she will catch us."

"You have forgotten the comb!" cried Martin. "Throw down the comb – quickly."

As soon as the comb touched the ground, a great thick hedge of brambles and thorns sprang up behind them. It seemed to stretch away into the distance as far as they could see. It was so broad and so tall that it looked like a vast stretch of thick forest.

When the witch came to it, she glowered with rage for it was too high for her broomstick and too thick for her to force a way through it. She tried, of course, and the sharp thorns scratched her face and tore at her cloak. Finally, with a shriek of fury, she turned her back on the hedge and set out for her miserable forest house.

The twins ran on and on until they reached their cottage and there, in the front garden, was their father.

"She wasn't a real granny at all!" the twins told him, as he hugged each of them in turn. "She was a terrible old witch!"

Their father was so angry with his wife when he heard what she had done that he chased her out of his home and told her never to come back. After that he didn't look for another new wife. Instead he did the housework himself, helped by the twins, and you may be sure they all lived happily together.

The Bold Little Tailor

THERE WAS once a little tailor who spent all his days stitch-ing, stitching, stitching. He made vests and jackets and trousers for all the grand men of the town. But although he worked so hard and although his stitches were strong and neat, the little tailor was very poor.

One beautiful summer morning, as he sat by his open window working away at a vest which had to be finished that day, the little tailor heard an old peasant woman crying her wares in the street below.

"Cherry jam! Fine, sweet cherry jam for sale!"

The little tailor put down his sewing and looked out of the window. He was in a merry, reckless mood that morning and he felt like treating himself. Besides, he was really quite hungry.

"I'll have some of your jam," he called down. "Bring your basket to my front door. I'll be with you right away."

And, whistling loudly, the little tailor ran down the stairs and opened his door.

The woman had big pots of cherry jam and small ones and it was

clear that she hoped very much that her new customer would buy
one of the big pots. But the little tailor knew that he could only
afford the very smallest pot of all and without much ado, that is just
what he picked out of her basket.

"Treat yourself, young master," wheedled the old woman, trying to hide her disappointment. "Go on – treat yourself to one of
the big pots."

But the little tailor could not be persuaded. He paid for the tiny
pot of jam, thanked the woman graciously, and closed his door
quickly.

Once back in his workshop, he went over to the cupboard and
got out a loaf of bread. Then he cut himself a large slice, and he
spread it all over with the rich, sweet-smelling cherry jam.

"I am going to enjoy this," he said to himself as he put the plate of
bread and jam on the table. "But first I must finish my vest. It
won't take long now." And he picked up his work and began
stitching again. This time, it must be admitted, his stitches were
perhaps not quite as neat as they had been, for already he was
thinking of how much he was going to enjoy his feast.

Meanwhile, the smell of the sweet jam was filling the tiny room. And before long, it attracted a swarm of flies which had settled on the ceiling. Down they came, buzzing round the bread and jam. They refused to be driven away, no matter how much the little tailor shouted at them.

"Shoo! Be off with you!" he exclaimed over and over again. "Pesky flies! Leave my jam alone!"

But the more the little man shouted and waved his arms, the more determined it seemed the flies became. Buzz-zz-z! Buzz-z-z-z! In another second they would be on his jam.

At last, in a rage, the little tailor seized a piece of cloth and began swiping at them. "Just you wait!" he yelled. "I'll finish you!"

And finish them he did – at least some of them. For when he looked down at the table, there lay seven flies, not buzzing anymore, but quite, quite dead.

"Well, I warned you, didn't I?" exclaimed the little tailor. And he puffed out his small chest. "Now I'm the champion! Goodness, gracious me! To put an end to seven of you – just like that. The town must hear of this. No, no, *not only* the town! The whole wide world!" Convinced of how clever he was and so proud of his

daring, suddenly it seemed to the little tailor he could no longer sit quietly toiling in his workshop, making vests and jackets and trousers.

Quickly he ate his bread and jam. Then he sat down and cut and sewed himself a broad belt. On it, he stitched the letters: SEVEN AT ONE BLOW.

"Now," he said, his eyes as bright as shiny buttons, "I'm ready to face the world! This small workshop is too humble a place for a hero such as I."

And with that, he fastened the belt round his tiny waist and then took out what food there was in his cupboard. In fact all that was there was a piece of stale, soft cheese, but, no matter, it would be something to eat on his travels. He looked about him for a moment and then ran down the stairs and out into the street.

In no time at all he had left the town behind him and was out in the country. Presently, as he walked briskly along, he saw a little brown bird struggling to disentangle itself from some bushes. So he freed it and put it in his pocket thinking it would be company for him.

Continuing on his way, he found the road led him up a great tall mountain. He climbed up and when he got to the very top – who should he find there but an enormous giant! The giant was sitting on a huge boulder and was looking about him as if he owned everything he saw.

The little tailor stared up at the giant for a long moment. Then he said cheerfully, "Good day, friend, I'm off on an adventure. You're welcome to come with me, if you will."

The giant could scarcely believe his ears when he heard this. And he peered down at the little man before him with the utmost contempt and scorn.

"Why you – you midget!" he spluttered finally. "Me – come with you? I could step on you and crush you as I would a beetle, if I so chose."

"That may be as you say," retorted the little tailor, unbuttoning his coat. "But read the words on my belt and you will learn from them just what kind of a man I am."

Very slowly, the giant read the words: SEVEN AT ONE BLOW – and thought, as he was meant to think, that the little man had killed seven men. He hid his surprise as best as he could, thinking that he would test the little man's strength for himself.

"Watch me," he roared, bending down and picking up a large stone which he began to squeeze as hard as he could.

The little tailor did watch and before long water ran out of the stone.

"That's nothing," he said, casually. "Now watch me." And taking the piece of stale cheese out of his pocket he squeezed it until moisture ran from it.

The giant, who was not only slow-witted but somewhat near-sighted, thought the little man was squeezing a stone. When he saw the moisture drop from it, he exclaimed, "Well done! But let me test you further."

With these words, he picked up another stone and flung it such a great distance that it almost vanished from sight.

"Very good," said the little tailor, leaning back, his arms folded. "But I will throw my stone so far that you won't ever see it come to earth."

He took the little brown bird out of his pocket and cast it into the air. Happy to be free, the bird soared away and was soon lost to sight.

"Hmm!" muttered the giant, overcome with astonishment. "Well, it may be that I have misjudged you after all. But let us have just one more trial of strength. Let us see if you are strong enough to carry that great oak over there."

And he strode over to the mighty tree and uprooted it with one hand.

"Of course," said the tailor cheerfully. "I suggest you take the trunk on your shoulder and I will take the heavier end which is surely the branches."

No sooner did the giant heave the trunk onto his shoulder than the tailor hopped in among the branches. The giant, of course, could not look round as he staggered along bearing the whole weight of the tree on his shoulder and the little man as well!

At last he let out a mighty groan. "I can go no further!" he gasped. As he dropped the trunk, the tailor hopped down quickly and when the giant looked round, the little man had his arms around some of the branches.

"You really do surprise me," said the little tailor with a merry smile. "I didn't think a giant like you would tire so easily."

"You surprise me!" exclaimed the giant, who was panting heavily. "I'd like you to come home with me to meet my brothers."

"I'd enjoy that very much," replied the tailor.

As they walked along, the giant suddenly took hold of the top of a cherry tree by the side of the road and pulled it down.

"Hold onto that," he told the little man, "I want to pick some cherries."

Now the little tailor could no more hold onto the branches than he could have squeezed water out of a stone and as they sprang back, he flew into the air with them.

"What!" roared the giant in amazement. "You cannot even hold down these few branches!"

"That's not true," retorted the tailor, who had landed neatly on his feet on the other side of the tree. "I simply chose to jump over the tree to avoid being shot at. I believe there are some hunters down in the valley with guns that they are pointing this way."

"If you can jump over the tree, then so can I," said the giant. But he was much too heavy to do anything of the kind and at his first attempt he found himself stuck fast in the branches. The little tailor, however, was wise enough to hide his amusement. When the giant had freed himself, he said, "I think we'll go straight home now. You can sleep the night in our cave."

The tailor was not at all frightened when, on reaching the cave, he saw two more giants, who were, if anything, bigger and fiercer-looking than his new friend. The giants made him welcome but, as he had no liking for the roast sheep which one of them had prepared for supper, the tailor said he wasn't hungry.

"Then you can sleep in that bed over there by the sacks," one of the brothers told him. "We will waken you at dawn."

But the giants changed their minds about this for as they talked they decided that the little tailor had made a fool of their brother and that he must die. Meanwhile, however, the little tailor, finding the bed much too big and hard to be comfortable, had slipped out of it. Instead he found a warm, dark corner as far away from the giants as possible and was soon sleeping soundly.

The giants waited until they thought the little tailor would be asleep; then one of them took a huge, heavy plank of wood and beat the bed very firmly with it.

"That's the end of him," said the first giant with a roar of laughter. "Now he will tell no stories of how he won every trial of strength against us giants." Then in the darkness of the cave, the

brothers stumbled about for a while, drinking and making merry, so pleased were they at having so easily rid themselves of the little man.

As soon as it was light and without even looking in the direction of the bed where, as they thought, the little tailor lay dead, they went out to hunt for their breakfast.

Meanwhile, the little tailor slept on in his corner. When he did open his eyes and looked around, he was quite disappointed to find that the giants had gone out. Nevertheless he felt he must make the best of things and, finding some cherries and some bread, he had a good breakfast. Then he left the cave.

As he walked along he was pleased to see the three giants coming towards him. But to the little tailor's astonishment, the giants gave loud roars of terror at the sight of him and then took to their heels, tripping each other up in their frantic efforts to get away from him.

"Now I wonder what has frightened them?" the little tailor asked

himself, as he went on down the road. "Ah well, perhaps that roast sheep they ate last night upset them."

By late morning the little tailor had reached what seemed to be a large and important town. He was feeling rather tired after his long walk and made his way to the royal palace, thinking that there he might at least receive a meal worthy of a hero. The sun was hot and the grass in the courtyard soft and green, and the little man, forgetting his hunger, could only think of taking a nap. He threw himself down on the grass, unbuttoned his jacket, and was soon sleeping soundly.

While he lay there a crowd came to stare at him and first one and then another read the words on his belt: SEVEN AT ONE BLOW.

"Seven at one blow!" a man exclaimed. "Why, we must be looking at a hero. The king himself should hear of this unknown warrior who is honoring our city with a visit."

The king, who was always afraid that one day he might have to fight a war to save his crown, was delighted to hear of such a champion within his kingdom. He sent his ambassador to wait upon the stranger and to invite him to join the army.

The little tailor was more than pleased to accept the king's offer –

especially when he was given a fine uniform to wear, a noble horse to ride and a suite of rooms all to himself in the royal palace.

But such favors made all the generals and courtiers extremely jealous of the little tailor. And in a very short time they went to the king and told him that if he did not find a way to rid himself of his new champion they would refuse to serve him.

The king did not know what to do. He had no great liking for the little man. In fact, secretly he was afraid of him, for if the warrior could kill seven men at one blow then almost certainly he would be able to destroy the king himself, should he become angry.

At last the king had a brilliant idea. In the forest, beyond the town, lived two very fierce and disagreeable giants. For a long time they had struck fear into the hearts of his people and, although once or twice he had sent his army against them, the soldiers had always run away when the giants began to fight. Now he would send his new champion against them. The giants would surely kill him and the king's worries would be over.

The very next day, the king sent for the little tailor.

"I have a task which I desire you to perform," the king said to him. "I want you to go into the forest and rid me of two terrible giants." So sure was he of what would happen he added, rather unwisely, "If you are successful you shall marry my daughter and have half my kingdom."

Now the tailor had seen the beautiful princess once or twice and was already more than half in love with her. She was certainly worth fighting two giants.

"I will do it," he said.

"Good," said the king. "Some of my soldiers will take you into the forest."

So the tailor and the soldiers set out for the forest that same day. But when they reached the edge of the forest, the little tailor sent the soldiers away. "I will fight the giants on my own and in my own way," he said with a great show of bravery. The soldiers were only too pleased to let him go on alone!

The little tailor ran off into the forest and before long, he found the two giants under a tree. One had a mop of red hair while the other's was black, and both were so sound asleep that their snores sounded like thunderclaps.

Filling both his pockets with stones, the little tailor climbed up into the tree and was soon astride one of its branches – one that hung

directly above the sleeping giants. When he had satisfied himself that he could hit each of the giants with the stones, the little man took the first one and dropped it on the red-haired giant. The giant did not move and the tailor dropped a few more stones which struck him on the head and chest.

At last, the giant opened his eyes sleepily and nudged his companion. "Leave me alone" he growled. "What's the matter with you? Let me sleep."

The tailor waited a moment, then he dropped more stones – this time on the giant with black hair. The black-haired giant woke almost at once and growled, "What do you want? This is no way to treat a friend."

"I didn't touch you," protested the first giant. "I can assure you I have done nothing."

"Oh yes, you did," returned the other. "Look at all these stones lying around. You've been pelting me with them."

They argued for a few minutes and then closed their eyes again in sleep. The tailor waited silently. After a while, he let fall his biggest stone. It struck the red-haired giant hard on the nose and he sprang up in rage. So, too, did his companion. And before you could say 'Jack Robinson,' the two giants were at each other's throats.

They fought each other as only giants can fight, using uprooted trees as clubs, and before long they were both stretched out on the ground – dead!

Smiling to himself, the little tailor hopped down from his tree, drew his sword and plunged it into the red-headed giant's chest and then into the black-haired giant. Then he went back to the edge of the forest where the soldiers, under their captain, were waiting for him.

"The giants are dead," he cried, waving his blood-stained sword. "But it was a fierce battle I can tell you. Take me back to the king so that I may give him the glad tidings."

When the king heard the news, he was far from pleased. He had no wish that his lovely daughter should marry such a common little man, and he certainly was not prepared to give away half his kingdom. After a great deal of tut-tutting and spluttering, he said at last, "There is just one more task I would ask you to perform before you claim your reward."

"What is it?" asked the tailor, thinking that the king was hard to please.

'There is a certain unicorn running wild in the forest," said the king. "Its single horn is more deadly than any sword. Capture it and half my kingdom and my daughter will be yours."

"That sounds easy enough," replied the champion. "Easy, that is for one who has killed seven at one blow."

The king smiled at this for the unicorn had killed a score of his knights and he had no doubt that it would make short work of the boastful little man standing before him.

But – once again – the king was greatly mistaken. The little tailor, with only his axe and a piece of stout rope for weapons, entered the dark forest fearlessly and began his search for the unicorn.

The wild beast and the hunter saw each other at the same moment. The unicorn immediately lowered its horn and plunged forward. The tailor waited for the beast to draw near, then skipped behind a tree. Unable to stop its headlong gallop, the unicorn ended up with its horn rammed into the trunk of the tree.

"Now, my fierce fellow, I have you!" cried the tailor, after he had made certain that the unicorn was stuck fast. And he wound his stout rope round the beast's neck before cutting the horn out of the tree with his axe.

Imagine the king's annoyance when that same day the tailor appeared at the palace leading the unicorn!

"Here is your dangerous unicorn," cried the tailor, before the king could speak. "I have earned my reward. Give me your daughter's hand in marriage and half your kingdom as you promised."

But the king was not going to give in so easily.

"You have done well – very well," he said smoothly, "but there is just one small favor you could do for me before you take your reward."

"What is it?" asked the tailor, hiding his anger.

"Well," began the king, "there is the question of the wild boar. For some time now my people have asked me to have it destroyed but, truth to tell, not one of my bravest knights will face it."

"Leave this boar to me!" cried the little tailor, thinking that his

brave words would make an impression on the lovely princess. "I will go into the forest this very day and seek it out."

And he ran from the palace. No sooner had he entered the forest than the boar made a rush at him from behind some bushes. And the little tailor was all but overcome by its flaying tusks. Indeed he only just had time to leap into a small chapel that was close by. The boar ran after him, but the tailor jumped out through the tiny window, skipped round the outside quickly and banged the door shut. The savage boar was, of course, much too fat and heavy to get through the window. So, again, the little tailor had captured the terrible animal without suffering a single scratch.

When he was sure that the boar could not possibly escape, the little man summoned some of the king's hunters to see his captive and to accompany him back to the palace.

The king was now obliged to keep his promise, and within a week his daughter became the tailor's bride.

The little tailor was now so happy that he could scarcely believe that he had ever suffered hard times. It was only at night, as he lay beside his lovely young wife, that he was sometimes caught up in dreadful nightmares. On one such night, the young princess heard

him shout, "Boy, fetch me a needle and thread. Stitch, stitch, stitch – I must finish this vest today."

Horrified, she left the bedchamber and went to her father.

"You have married me to a common little tailor," she wept. "Oh, father, what must we do to get rid of him?"

Her father consoled her as well as he could. Then he said, "I dare not risk his anger for we know he can kill seven at one blow. But tomorrow night, as he sleeps, my soldiers will bind his hands and feet and carry him to one of our ships. The ship will take him to the other side of the world and that will be the end of him!"

The next day the princess confided their plan to her lady-in-waiting, but the young woman felt so sorry for her master that she ran to him and told him the whole dreadful plot.

That night the little tailor only pretended to be asleep and dreaming. And presently, as the soldiers waited outside the bedchamber, they heard him call out, "Boy, fetch your needle and thread. Stitch, stitch – I must have this vest finished today or I will have your head. Have I not killed two giants, slaughtered a fierce unicorn and trapped a wild boar . . ."

When the soldiers heard these words they began to tremble at the knees and, finally, they rushed away as one man!

In the morning, the tailor declared that he had enjoyed an excellent sleep and his young wife, thinking now that she had been mistaken and hurried in her judgment, kissed him tenderly and vowed that he was the best and the noblest of husbands.

Rapunzel

ONCE UPON a time, when there were more witches in the world than you could possibly imagine, there lived one whose pride and joy was her garden.

No one in the neighborhood dared to venture near this witch for she was known to have an evil nature and a very spiteful tongue and, besides, she had built a high stone wall around her house and garden to keep out all intruders.

Living right next door to this terrible old woman was a young couple whose back window looked down into her garden. For a long time the young people had longed to have a child and when at last the wife was able to tell her husband that their wish was to come true, they were both indescribably happy.

Time passed joyously for them until one day the husband, whose name was Jacob, came home from work to find his wife staring out of the back window.

"What's the matter?" he asked anxiously for she looked pale and ill. "Why are you staring down into the witch's garden?"

"She has a patch of the most delicious-looking radishes growing there," replied the young wife, without taking her eyes from the

garden. "I long for a taste of radishes so much that I fear I will pine away if I do not have some."

"But you know I dare not ask the old witch for anything," Jacob protested, in horror. "I will do anything for you – anything, but that!"

"Then I will die," said the young wife turning to him, "for I cannot live without them."

When Jacob saw that his wife meant what she said, he was very upset and frightened. "To ask the witch is impossible," he told himself. "But supposing I wait until it is dark and climb over the wall. Then I could help myself to some of the radishes. Surely she will not miss a few."

Without telling his wife, Jacob did just that, and when he returned with the radishes and gave them to her, he saw how her eyes lit up and the color came back into her cheeks. Even as she ate them, she seemed to grow stronger and more like her usual self.

All went well for a few days until one evening Jacob returned home to find her once again staring down at the witch's garden.

"Oh, no," he cried. "Don't ask me to steal the witch's radishes for you again."

"I shall die if I do not have them," whispered his young wife, tearfully.

And on seeing how pale and ill she looked Jacob knew there was nothing else for it. He had to climb the high wall once again and take some of the radishes.

As before, Jacob was lucky, and he was soon back home safely, clutching a handful of the rosy red vegetables.

"I saw nothing of the old witch," he told his wife cheerfully. "Now make yourself a salad and enjoy them. You will soon feel better."

But far from being satisfied, no sooner had the young wife finished the radishes than she began to protest that she must be able to look forward to more the next day.

"I must have some," she declared. "I must! These are so good that my desire for them is stronger than ever."

"Very well," said Jacob at last, after he had tried to dissuade her. "I will climb the wall once more. But if the witch comes out and catches me – well, I just dare not think what she will do."

But Jacob was to find out, for the third time he climbed the high wall, his luck ran out. The witch was waiting for him!

"So it is you who has been stealing my precious radishes, is it?" she cackled, her red eyes ablaze with spite and malice. "You shall suffer for it – thief that you are."

Jacob tried in vain to beg for mercy and understanding, pointing out there were still lots of radishes left for the witch. But the old crone simply increased her threats, finally saying she would bind him in her service for a hundred years.

The poor man's blood ran cold at the idea and he cried, "But, don't you understand – I was afraid that if my wife did not have the radishes, she might lose the child we are expecting."

"Ah-ha," shrieked the witch. "So that is it! Promise me this child and I will let you go. And more – you may take as many radishes as you need to satisfy your wife."

Terrified out of his wits and ready to agree to anything that would free him, Jacob stammered, "Yes, yes, you may take the child." And so the witch let him go.

Soon afterwards, his wife gave birth to a beautiful baby girl, and the very next day the witch appeared and claimed the child.

"I will bring her up as if she were my own," she said, with a wicked cackle, gathering the child up in her arms. "But you shall never set eyes on her again."

The witch, who was called Gotel – a name ugly enough to suit her – christened the baby Rapunzel. As soon as the little girl could speak, the witch taught her to call her Mother Gotel.

When Rapunzel was twelve or thirteen years old, she was the loveliest girl under the sun, and the witch decided that no man should ever look at her. Using her magic powers, she placed Rapunzel in a high tower which had neither stairs, nor doors, in the middle of a forest.

"Here you must stay, my pretty," she told the girl. "But I will come each afternoon to visit you. When you hear me call 'Rapunzel, Rapunzel let down your hair,' fasten your long braid to the hook in the window and I will climb up it like a rope ladder."

The years passed. Rapunzel, alone in her high tower, grew more and more beautiful, but how long the days were! Mother Gotel visited her faithfully each afternoon and sometimes she would ask Rapunzel to sing to her.

One day, just after the witch had left Rapunzel, a handsome young Prince came riding through the forest. He was curious when he saw the high tower and then surprised to hear the sound of singing coming from its topmost window. So sad and sweet was the song that as he listened, the Prince found himself longing to see its singer. Although he searched for a long time, he could find neither stairs, nor door, nor entrance of any kind that would let him into the tower. At last he rode reluctantly away.

But the memory of the song haunted the young Prince and later that week he rode into the forest for a second time. Again he heard a girl's voice singing but this time as he listened from behind a tree, he saw a bent old woman with hooked nose and crooked back approach the tower. Then he heard the old woman say, "Rapunzel, Rapunzel, let down your hair."

To the Prince's surprise he saw a long braid of hair as fine as spun gold come down from the topmost window of the tower. Even more surprised he watched the old woman grasp it and climb slowly upwards.

"So that is the way to enter this mysterious tower," said the Prince to himself. "Tomorrow I will see what I can do."

Just as it was growing dark on the following day, the Prince arrived at the tower and got down from his horse. "Rapunzel, Rapunzel, let down your hair," he called softly, and almost at once, down came the shining braid of hair. The Prince grasped it and climbed upwards.

Rapunzel was terrified at the sight of the young man, for the only

person in her life that she had seen or spoken to was Mother Gotel. But the prince, seeing how frightened she was, spoke very gently.

"How beautiful you are," he said. "Let us be friends. Tell me your story – what power is it that keeps you here in this high tower?"

And, gradually, Rapunzel lost her fear of the handsome Prince. Soon she had told him the story of her life, such as it was, and how, each afternoon, Mother Gotel came to see her.

"Then I must come in the evening," declared the Prince when she had finished. "Do not try to prevent me, for already I have lost my heart to you."

The weeks went by. Each night, at dusk, the Prince visited Rapunzel, and all the time the witch suspected nothing. By now Rapunzel had given her heart to the young man and had promised – somehow – to be his wife.

"Oh, how shall I ever escape from this tower!" Rapunzel exclaimed on one of his visits. "I have thought about it much and now I think there is only one way. Each time you come you must bring me skeins of silk so that I can weave them into a rope."

The Prince brought silk on his next visit and Rapunzel set to work. She was careful to hide the silken rope as soon as she heard Mother Gotel's voice.

All went well for some time until, one fateful day, as the witch sat while my Prince is with me in the twinkling of an eye?"
Mother Gotel, how is it that you take so long to climb upwards, while my Prince is with me in the twinkling of an eye."

"What's this I hear!" shrieked the witch, her eyes glittering with rage. "Wicked, wicked child! You have deceived me. Never, never will I forgive you."

And, trembling with anger, she seized a pair of scissors and, snip, snap, she cut off the long shining gold braid. Rapunzel wept bitterly, but the witch merely struck her forcefully knocking her to the ground. Then, using her magic powers once again, she carried the girl off to a desert place and left her there.

That day just as it was growing dark, the Prince came as usual to the tower.

"Rapunzel, Rapunzel, let down your hair," he called softly, as he always did, and down came the long braid. But when he climbed quickly upwards, he found not his dear Rapunzel waiting for him, but the ugly, angry witch. Cunningly she had fastened Rapunzel's golden braid to the hook, knowing that this was the only way to entice the king's son into the tower.

"So you thought to steal my child, did you!" she cackled, her cruel eyes staring at him in spiteful triumph. "Ah, but your little love, your dove, has flown. You will never find her – never, never see her again."

And with a dreadful high-pitched laugh, she advanced on the bewildered young man, scratching his face with her nails and pushing him, with tremendous force, out of the window.

The Prince fell, down, down, down – coming to land in a bush full of sharp thorns. As he fell face down the thorns pierced his eyes, blinding him. Helpless, he stumbled into the forest, and unable as he was to find his way home, there he remained for many a long month, keeping himself alive on the berries and roots which grew there. Never, for one moment did he forget his beloved Rapunzel. When it seemed that food was growing scarce in the forest, the poor blind beggar – as he now was – took to wandering further and further afield. Finally, without knowing it, he came to the desert place where Rapunzel now lived.

Rapunzel, lonely and unhappy, saw the poor man stumbling towards her one day as she sat dreaming of her Prince. But love is a powerful thing and the love that Rapunzel bore inside her told her in an instant that this miserable beggar was none other than her Prince. She called out to him and the Prince, recognizing her voice, lifted his head and held out his arms.

Falling upon his neck, Rapunzel began to weep without restraint and it was then that the final miracle happened. Her clear, warm tears bathed the Prince's poor blind eyes, until, little by little, his sight returned.

With the lovely Rapunzel at his side, the Prince made his way back to his father's kingdom where, amid great rejoicings, their marriage was celebrated by everyone.

The royal pair lived happily from that day on and their love for each other was so strong that the wicked witch could never harm them again.

Jack and the Beanstalk

A VERY LONG time ago, there lived a poor farmer's widow. She was really very poor indeed; all she had in the world was a son called Jack and a cow called Daisy-bell.

Jack did what he could to make his mother's life easier but he was somewhat easygoing and not very hard-working. He had a cheerful way of saying, "Don't worry, mother, everything will turn out all right, you'll see," which generally made his mother rather cross.

"Everything will not turn out all right, Jack," she said to him one morning, weeping and wringing her hands after he had come out with his usual remark. "We haven't even got money enough to pay the rent and you know what that means."

"We still have Daisy-bell," said Jack, cheerful as ever. "She gives us milk and what's left over fetches a good price at the market."

"Even if we had ten Daisy-bells, we still couldn't manage to find enough for the rent right now," said his mother. "No, Jack, I've made up my mind. Daisy-bell must go. You will have to take her to market and sell her. That is the only way we shall get enough money together for the landlord."

Jack was very fond of the good-natured cow and, when he saw

that his mother really meant what she said, he began to protest. But his mother cut him short.

"This morning," she said in a firm voice. "This very morning, you will take Daisy-bell to market, and see that you get a good price for her. Now that's my last word on the matter."

So as soon as Jack had eaten his breakfast, he fetched Daisy-bell from the tiny paddock and set out for market. He hadn't gone very far down the road when he saw a very odd-looking little man coming towards him. He was small and bent and walked slowly but, when he drew level with Jack, the boy saw that his eyes were as sharp as needles and very bright.

"Good morning, Jack," said the little man.

"And to you too," said Jack, wondering how the stranger knew his name.

"And where are you off to so early today?" asked the man.

"As a matter of fact," said Jack, not really liking the question very much, "I'm going to the market to sell my cow." He held on-to Daisy-bell's halter more firmly as he added, "But what is that to you, may I ask?"

"Everything," replied the stranger, and his eyes danced and twinkled, "for, you see, I have a mind to buy your cow and so save you the journey to market."

"How much will you offer?" asked Jack suspiciously. "You don't look like a farmer in need of a fine cow like Daisy-bell here."

"I'll give you – " here the little man paused.

"Well?" demanded Jack impatiently.

"I'll give you five beans," went on the little man. And he drew out of his pocket five very strange-looking beans.

Jack could scarcely believe his ears. First he laughed and then he grew angry. He shook his head and finally he shouted, "Goodness me, you must take me for a fool! My Daisy-bell – for these queer-looking beans! Never!"

"Ah," said the little man, not in the least upset at Jack's outburst. "You don't understand, although I wouldn't say you were a stupid fellow. These are no ordinary beans, Jack. They're magic! Would you turn down the offer of five magic beans when they are worth a hundred times the value of your cow? Take my word for it!"

"I don't believe you!" exclaimed Jack, but his voice was quieter and less confident as he stared at the beans. "Magic, you say?"

"Magic they are," repeated the little man. "And if you take them

and plant them in your garden tonight, you'll find that in the morning they will have grown right up to the sky."

"And supposing I did strike such a bargain," Jack said. "And supposing they didn't grow up to the sky – would you give me back the cow?"

"Certainly," said the stranger, at once, "I give you my word."

Jack hesitated for a while. But the idea of becoming the owner of five magic beans took hold of his imagination. And magic beans must surely be more worthwhile than money!

Suddenly, he laughed loudly. "I'll take them," he cried. "Give me your magic beans, little man. And here, you take Daisy-bell."

He handed over the cow's halter to the little man, who made off down the road leading Daisy-bell without a backward glance.

It was late afternoon before Jack could finally bring himself to go back home for he was more than a little anxious at what his mother would have to say. She would be furious, he supposed. Finally telling himself not to worry and whistling a merry tune, he opened the cottage door and went inside.

"You're back earlier than I expected," said his mother. "But never mind. Tell me how much money you got for Daisy-bell. Is it enough for the rent? Well, speak up, Jack."

"I didn't sell the cow for money," Jack began. "I – I sort of exchanged her. But what a bargain I made. Look, mother!" And he threw the five magic beans on the table. "They're magic, real magic, and . . ."

He got no further for his mother had seized the mophead and was trying, in vain, to hit him with it. Then she sank down onto a chair and covered her face with her hands, crying as if her heart would break. This lasted only a moment, however – she was on her feet again in a trice, pounding Jack with her hands and screaming, "Idiot, fool, donkey! Do you know what you've done? Now we shall have to leave our home! Oh, Jack! And as for your magic beans! This is what I think of them . . ." She scooped them up off the table and threw them out of the window.

"Mother, please don't worry . . ." Jack began, trying to sound cheerful. But his mother was too angry to listen to anything he had to say. She pushed him out of the kitchen, shouting, "Off to bed with you this instant! You can whistle for your supper for there'll be none provided by me! Off with you!"

Tired and hungry, Jack went to bed, but not to sleep. He still believed his beans were magic and he was miserable at the loss of them. "Plant them," the little man had said. But his mother had given him no chance. She had thrown them out of the window and now they would be lying among the weeds with all their magic going out of them.

But Jack was wrong, for as he lay in his bed thinking about them, the magic beans were taking root. And they were growing – and growing. By the time Jack got up and dressed, they were on their way to the sky.

"That's why my room is so dark!" Jack exclaimed, as he stared at the great tall beanstalk in astonishment. "My beans have taken root and now they're growing up to the sky. They *were* magic."

The beanstalk had grown up so close to Jack's window that it was the easiest thing in the world for him to jump onto the ladder-like stalks and begin climbing upwards. And this is just what he did.

On and upwards he climbed, up and up, until at last he reached the sky. There, stretching before him, was a long straight road which just seemed to cry out to Jack to walk along it. And Jack did, his heart pounding with excitement and curiosity. The road was certainly long, but he felt no tiredness – only a dreadful hunger, having missed both his supper and his breakfast.

So he walked on and on, not knowing how far he had been or how much further he would go, until at last he came to a huge, tall, gray, castle-like house. The woman on the doorstep was more than twice his own size, but still Jack walked up to her.

"Good morning, ma'am," he said, politely. "Could you let me have something to eat, please? I'm faint with hunger."

"You don't want to come here asking for food," said the woman, although not unkindly. "My husband is a fierce giant, and I've known him make a meal out of a lad like you."

"If he's not at home," said Jack, "I could just nip into your kitchen, ma'am, for a bite and then nip out again. I wouldn't be more than a moment, but truly, I'm starving hungry."

The big woman scratched her head in a doubtful way. She liked little Jack's manner and she was lonely, but she knew what her husband's appetite could be like.

"Very well," she said. "But you had better be quick about it."

Jack followed her into an immense kitchen and soon he had sat down to thick slices of bread and cheese and a bowl of milk. But just as he was beginning on his second slice, the whole house began to tremble.

Thump, thump, thump! The noise of the heavy footsteps was like thunder. Jack jumped up from his chair, and the woman gasped, "Mercy upon us! It's my husband! What shall I do now? Quick, hide in the oven!" So saying, she opened the oven door and pushed Jack inside.

No sooner was the mighty giant in the kitchen than he shouted loudly and rudely for food. Straightaway his wife hurried off to get the calf which she had roasted for him the previous night. But before she could put it down in front of him, he began sniffing the air. Then he roared,

"Fee-fi-fo-fum,
I smell the blood of an Englishman,
Be he alive, or be he dead,
I'll grind his bones to make my bread."

"Nonsense, my love," said his wife, soothingly. "You must be mistaken. You can see for yourself there is no stranger here."

The giant lowered his great body into his own special chair, which was large enough to hold ten grown men, and began to eat greedily. When he had finished, he pushed the huge plate away and called impatiently for his bags of gold to be brought to him, so that he could count them as he always did each morning. His wife brought them thankfully, for she knew that it wouldn't be long before her husband would grow sleepy with the effect of his huge meal and the effort of counting.

Sure enough, the giant was soon fast asleep, and the woman tiptoed to the oven. "He's asleep now," she whispered to Jack. "Go away from here as fast as you can and don't come back."

Jack crept out of the oven and made for the door, but as he was passing the giant, he quickly and quietly helped himself to one of the bags of gold.

Down the long straight road he ran until he came to the beanstalk.

"Watch out, mother!" he yelled mischievously, as he let drop the bag of gold, which he knew would land in his mother's garden. Then he climbed down, down, down after it as fast as he could.

"Well, mother, those magic beans have not played us false," said Jack, as he put the bag of gold on the table. "Look, there is enough gold here to live on for many a long day."

"I was wrong about the beans," admitted his mother. "And I'm sorry. But that giant up in the sky sounds like a dangerous fellow, and I think he's best left alone. So give up any idea of climbing the beanstalk again, Jack. It's too risky."

Well, for a time, Jack was content to stay at home. But when all the gold was finished, he began to think more and more about the giant and to wonder what other treasures he kept up there in his castle in the sky.

Early one fine summer morning Jack rose early, went silently downstairs and out into the garden. He had decided to climb the beanstalk again, without telling his mother. And so he began climbing, up and up. And there, at the top was the long straight road, and at the end of it was the huge, tall, gray, castle-like house, just as he remembered it all. There, too, was the woman on the doorstep, still twice as large as he.

"Good morning, ma'am," said Jack, brightly and boldly. "Could you spare me a bite to eat for I'm really starving hungry."

"Go away!" cried the woman when she saw him. "When my husband catches you he will have you for his breakfast."

"Ah," said Jack knowingly. "But he's not in at the moment, is he? So there would be time for me to have something to eat – if you can spare it, please," he added politely.

The woman hesitated. She longed to have somebody to talk to and besides she wanted to question Jack about the missing bag of gold. After a moment she nodded her head. "Come on, then."

But Jack had scarcely sat down to eat before – *thump, thump,*

thump, the whole house began to tremble and shake violently.

This time, without being told, Jack hopped into the oven just seconds before the mighty giant thudded into the kitchen.

All happened as before. The giant sniffed the air and roared "Fee-fi-fo-fum," as he had done the last time. But his wife was so quick in producing the roasted oxen and setting it before him that he forgot his suspicions and began to eat.

Then he called, "Wife, bring me my little hen that lays the golden eggs." Immediately she fetched it and set it down before him.

The hen laid an egg of purest gold as it sat there. The giant nodded his head contentedly and blinked. Then he gave a great wide yawn and was soon fast asleep.

As before Jack crept out of the oven, but as he made for the door, he caught hold of the wonderful hen and made off with it. The hen, however, had a voice of its own; it cackled so loudly it woke the giant.

Jack was halfway down the long, straight road before the giant had gathered his wits sufficiently to come thundering after him. Jack was lighter too and was able to outrun him and, in no time at all, he was climbing down the beanstalk with his prize. When Jack was safely inside his own kitchen, he called his mother and showed

her the hen. Then he cried, "Lay," and the hen laid an egg of pure gold.

"Now we can sell these gold eggs whenever we need money," Jack told his mother. "Our worries are over."

"And I hope that makes you content to stay at home," said his mother, "for – mark my words – you won't always be so lucky."

But Jack couldn't forget about the giant and his treasures at his castle in the sky. "Just once more," he told himself, as he stared up at the beanstalk one day. "I must climb you just once more."

When Jack came in sight of the castle-like house for the third time and saw the woman on the doorstep he was too clever to show himself to her. "She certainly won't invite me inside again," he thought. So he waited until he saw the giant's wife go into the courtyard, leaving the kitchen door wide open. Then, not wasting a moment, he ran straight to the door and slipped inside. There was no time to make for the oven, so this time he hid in the great shining copper pot where the woman boiled her dirty clothes.

It was not long before he heard the *thump, thump, thump* of the giant's heavy footsteps and felt the house tremble and shake. Then he heard the giant roar,

"Fee-fi-fo-fum,
I smell the blood of an Englishman.
Be he alive, or be he dead,
I'll grind his bones to make my bread."

Then Jack heard his wife say, "Now that's a real stupid remark, husband dear. I can assure you there's no stranger in my kitchen. You must still have the scent of that lad you ate for supper in your nostrils. Come, eat and then you can take your nap."

But before the giant fell asleep, he called, "Wife, bring me my golden harp." And she fetched it and set it down before him.

"Play for me!" ordered the giant, and by itself the harp played the most beautiful music. It played until the giant fell fast asleep.

When Jack heard the giant's loud snores he lifted the lid of the copper pot and crept, as quiet as a mouse, to the table. Then he grabbed hold of the golden harp and ran with it to the door. But like the little hen, the harp too had a voice of its own and it began calling, "Master! Master!"

This time the giant woke up instantly, in time to see Jack disappearing through the door. With a great roar of anger, he got to his feet and set off in hot pursuit.

What a chase that was! Jack couldn't hope to outrun the giant this time, but he had had a fair start and, moreover, he took care to watch where he was going, while the giant, almost blinded with rage, kept falling and stumbling.

When Jack reached the top of the beanstalk, he swung himself down from branch to branch like a monkey. "Mother, mother!" he shouted as he reached the ground. "Quick, fetch me the axe. The giant is not far behind."

Shivering with fright, his mother brought him the axe and Jack swung it with all his strength against the beanstalk. The beanstalk began to sway; and Jack chopped at it again and again. At last it came crashing down and with it fell the mighty giant.

"Well, that's the end of the giant," said Jack calmly. "He will never rise again." Then he showed his mother the golden harp and commanded it to play.

At the sound of the beautiful melody, the widow forgave her reckless son, and they lived together for a long time in great comfort – thanks to the hen's golden eggs.

Jack grew so rich that he attracted the attention of a lovely Princess and, soon afterwards, married her. But, taking his mother's advice, he told her nothing of the magic beans and the beanstalk that had given him the chance to make his fortune.

The Wee Man of the Moors

THERE WAS once a young man called Tom. A farmer's boy he was, and not very fond of hard work. His master was a rich landowner, with a farm that stretched to the edge of the wild lonely moorland and horses in his stables that were fit for a king to ride.

Tom's duties on the farm were many and varied. One day he would be grooming the horses, another day – cleaning the farm implements and on yet another feeding the hens. He could be described as a "Jack-of-all-trades and master of none." And if you are wondering why Tom had no special skills, it was because he had no special interest in anything he did. He did just what he had to do and no more, and if his work was good enough to keep him on friendly terms with his fellow-workers and earn him his wages, he was content.

Instead of studying or reading books in his free time, Tom would go tramping about over the moors. Sometimes he would sit idly by the edge of a small pool which was far off the beaten track.

It was here one day that he had watched the baby moorhen struggle out of its shell and dive into the water when it was just five minutes old. And it was to this, his secret pool, that he returned time after time.

One bright summer Sunday, Tom set out for his afternoon walk, and as usual he made for the pool. He was very close to it when he suddenly heard a cry so shrill and plaintive that he stopped dead in his tracks. Slowly he looked about him.

What could it be? Where had it come from? Most of the birds' calls he knew, but this shrill wailing sound was unlike any of them. Indeed, it was more like the crying of a baby in distress than anything else, but there was certainly no baby in sight.

Tom began searching among the undergrowth, kicking up the turf, and pulling aside great clumps of tough grass with his hands. At the same time he cursed softly under his breath at this unexpected interruption to his Sunday outing.

Finding nothing in his search, he got down on his hands and knees and put his ear to the ground. As he listened, it seemed to him that he could just make out some words mingling with the sobs.

"What's that? What do you say?" Tom shouted.

"The big stone! Oh, oh, oh! The big stone is on top!"

"What big stone?" Tom shouted again. "On top of what?" He crawled towards the pond and suddenly, he saw by its edge a huge, flat stone half buried in the mud, almost hidden by weeds.

Tom got to his feet and went up to the stone, certain now that whatever it was that was sobbing and wailing so pathetically was trapped underneath that stone.

"Lift the stone, lift the stone," came the high-pitched voice.

Tom hesitated no longer. He began straining at the stone with all his young strength, pushing and tugging and gasping with the effort. At last the stone came up out of the damp earth with a squelchy, sucking sound that sent shivers down Tom's broad back.

He wiped the sweat from his brow and then peered into the hole. What he saw lying there made him catch his breath, for he was looking down at a wee man who had a face as brown and wrinkled as a piece of old parchment and a yellow beard so long that it had wrapped itself about the wee man's body like a sheet.

With unbelieving eyes Tom just stared and stared. At last he found his tongue sufficiently to stammer, "I'm – I'm sorry, s-sir, that it took me such a time to – er – set you free."

"I was very nearly finished," said the wee man in a high-pitched, piping voice, and his black eyes glittered like diamonds in his wrinkled face. "But I won't forget you, Tom, not ever. For if you

hadn't removed the stone, I would have stayed there for eternity."

Then he sprang from the hole with so much energy that Tom took a step backwards in alarm and all but toppled into the pool.

"Lord save us!" he exclaimed. "You're – you're a bogle!"

"That I am not!" declared the wee man. "Hobgoblin I may be, but bogle – never!"

"Well, whatever you are," said Tom more calmly now, "you're not of my kind. And, if it please you, sir, I'll be on my way back to the farm, where there is work to be done."

"Don't go yet, Tom," said the hobgoblin, "for I am in your debt, and I must repay you. Ask me a favor. Ask it quickly and it will be granted as soon as you've named it."

"I can't – can't think . . ." Tom began uneasily.

"What about a beautiful young wife to warm your slippers," suggested the wee man. "She's yours if you but say so. I'll find you the best in the land and see that she takes good care of you."

"No, no – not that," said Tom hastily. "I've never been one for the girls and in my opinion a man is better off without a wife."

"What about a bag of gold, then?" said the hobgoblin. "No, not one bag – ten . . ."

"That would be pleasant enough," Tom said, without much

enthusiasm. "But where is there to spend so much money in these parts? And what would I spend it on?"

"No wife, no gold!" snapped the hobgoblin, frowning and suddenly looking wickedly fierce. "What would you like then?"

Tom scratched his head. What indeed?

"Supposing I helped you with your work on the farm," said the hobgoblin. "Give you all your time to do as you like."

"Well, now you're talking!" cried Tom. "Why, I could spend my days on the moors, just wandering happily around . . ."

"Then that's it!" said the wee man. "The favor is granted and the debt is paid. But remember, Tom, if ever you should take it into your head to thank me – you will see me no more. I'll have no thanks. Is that clear?"

"It's clear," said Tom. "Will I see you again, sir?"

"Only if you call me," said the hobgoblin. "All you have to do is shout, 'Wee man of the moors come to me,' and I'll be with you."

Before Tom could ask any further questions, the wee man picked a dandelion and blew upon it with such vigor that a thick cloud of its fluffy parachutes floated into Tom's eyes. When he had brushed them away so he could see again, the wee man had vanished.

Tom pinched himself to make sure he hadn't been dreaming before setting off for the farm. When he got back, he told his mates

that he would do the dirtiest jobs on the farm the next morning if they would collect the hens' eggs for him. Not surprisingly, they agreed! Then Tom ate a healthy meal and went early to bed.

The next morning he got up at cockcrow so as to get through as much work as possible before the other farmhands appeared. The memory of the wee man of the moors had almost faded from his mind as he went first to muck out the stables.

Great was his astonishment to find that the job had already been done for him and much more thoroughly than he would ever have done it. The horses too were already groomed, their coats gleaming and shining. Then to his ever growing amazement, he found that the cows had been milked, the farm implements cleaned and polished till they glinted in the early morning sunshine like new; the chickens fed and the buckets filled.

"It's the hobgoblin's doing for certain," Tom told himself gleefully. "He has certainly kept his bargain."

Well, from that time onwards Tom had nothing to do. His master praised him for the brisk and efficient way his jobs were done and Tom told no one of the hobgoblin.

After a week or so of his new leisure, Tom found himself longing to catch a glimpse of the wee man of the moors at work, and so he took to wandering about the farm in the night hours. Every now and then, especially on nights when the moon was full, he would catch a glimpse or two of the hobgoblin in the yard or in the stable. Never a word did they exchange as the wee man hopped, like a will-o'-the-wisp, from one chore to the next.

Now, although all Tom's tasks were perfectly done, things went very differently for the other laborers on the farm. If Tom's buckets were full in the mornings, as often as not theirs had been tipped over into the mud. Tools they had carefully sharpened and put away the night before were found to be blunt and rusted in the morning and no use for anything.

Before very long Tom's fellow-workers began to look at him suspiciously. Whenever he tried to crack a joke with them or sit down at the table with them they would turn away and ignore him. By the end of the month not one of them would come near him and so convinced were they that Tom was the cause of all their misfortunes that they started to tell spiteful tales of him to their master.

"We've seen him in the dark hours of night wandering about the farm," they said. "He is up to no good."

Good-natured Tom was greatly upset by the behavior of his one-time friends and just to prove that he was willing to work, he took up a broom and began sweeping. But no sooner did he have it in his grasp than it danced away from him as if bewitched. It was the same story with every task he tried to do.

"This must be the wee man's doing," Tom told himself miserably. "He won't let me work. And what's more he's ruining everybody else's work about the farm."

Things got worse for Tom, and one day his master sent for him.

"I'm sorry it has come to this, Tom," he said. "But if I don't get rid of you the others will leave. Here's an extra week's wages. Now get your belongings and be away from here before nightfall."

Tom was dismayed for he had no wish to leave the farm. Above all, he was furious with the hobgoblin.

"Said he was doing me a favor, did he!" he muttered as he walked down the road. "And look what's happened. I've gotten fired for nothing at all. At least nothing that I've done myself."

And he worked himself up into such a fury that he suddenly shouted, "Wee man of the moors come to me! Come to me!"

Scarcely were the words out of his mouth than the hobgoblin appeared. Tom looked down at him angrily. He was too full of his own rage and disappointment to be scared of the wee man's wizened face and wicked, glinting black eyes.

"I'll thank you," Tom yelled, "I'll thank you to leave me alone. I don't want your help. I'll do my own work in the future."

So angry was he that he longed to give the wee man a shaking.

"You've said it, Tom!" the wee man screeched, pointing a brown finger at him. "You've thanked me and I told you not to."

"I'll thank you if I please," Tom muttered, a bit taken aback now by the creature's threatening voice. "Just leave me alone."

"That's the one thing I will never do," retorted the wee man. "I'll never *help* you again, Tom. But I'll never leave you alone."

"It was me that saved you from under that stone," Tom said. "Don't forget that!"

"I'll not forget that," said the wee man in his shrill piping voice. "Never – for as long as I was under the stone it was not in my power to do any man mischief."

"You mean it's in your nature to go about doing mischief to good folk?" Tom asked, beginning to wish that he had never summoned the creature.

"I do, I do," came the reply. "Especially fools, Tom. Fools like yourself. From now on I'll not work for you, but I will undo everything you try to do." The little hobgoblin gave a loud, screeching, mocking laugh that made Tom shiver.

Then the wee man, grimacing in a manner that nearly scared poor Tom out of his wits, began whirling and capering around him. His yellow beard rose like a curtain blown by the wind, until it was all about Tom, almost suffocating him.

"You'll not forget me, fool Tom," came the wee man's voice as if from a distance. "I'll be with you when there is work to be done and work to be undone!"

And with that, the yellow mists that had encircled Tom's head vanished and he found himself alone and trembling all over.

Well, it all came about just as the wee man of the moors had foretold. Tom drifted from one job to the next and whatever he tried to do was undone. No horse stayed groomed, no stable remained mucked out. Tools, cleaned and sharpened by Tom, were rusted and blunt within seconds. And worst of all every farmer that gave him work suffered some terrible disaster.

Thus it was that the wee man of the moors wreaked his spite and his vengeance on poor Tom until the day came when Tom gave up all idea of work and took to the roads, to live like a gypsy, when for a coin or two, he would tell his story to anyone who would listen.